cHARLie ThE Wiener Wonder Dog

By Cindy S. Brumbaugh

First Edition

PAGE PUBLISHING, INC.
New York, NY

First originally published by Page Publishing, Inc. 2015

ISBN 978-1-68289-615-0 (pbk)
ISBN 978-1-68139-883-9 (digital)

Printed in the United States of America

This book is dedicated to Benjamin and Bryan.
Never stop "*wondering*".
Besides your Dad, you two are my greatest loves!
And for Mom and Pop, my parents for 56 years!

And for Erica Jane Brumbaugh Massa. Whose light was taken from us too soon but shines more brilliantly in heaven.

Once upon a not-so-very-long time ago, there was a dachshund (pronounced: "doxon") named Charlie. Now Charlie lived with Bessie and Pete McDurgle on a small farm in Beagleville. However, Charlie did not always live with Bessie and Pete in Beagleville. Charlie used to live in the big city. During most of his early days, Charlie would be lying in his crate, dreaming of the green grass, chasing squirrels, and watching over the birds.

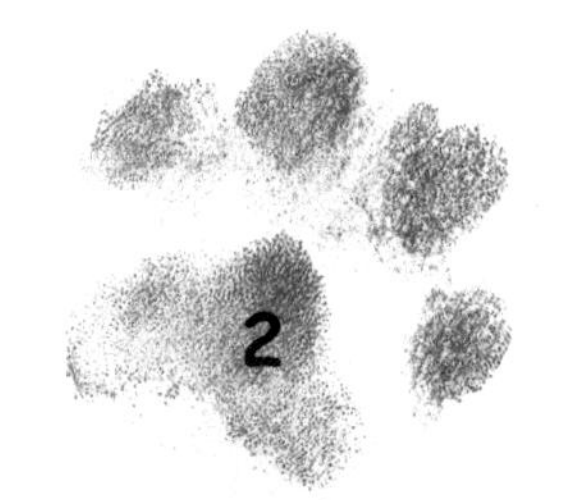

On an early spring day, Charlie's owners decided that they needed to move. They could not take Charlie with them. This made Charlie very sad.

"Where will I go?" he cried!

Not to worry because Charlie's big city owners called their friends—the McDurgles in Beagleville—and asked Bessie and Pete to look after him.

"We would love to take Charlie in," said Bessie and Pete! Bessie and Pete were a bit older. Their children and other pets had grown and moved away from the family farm in Beagleville.

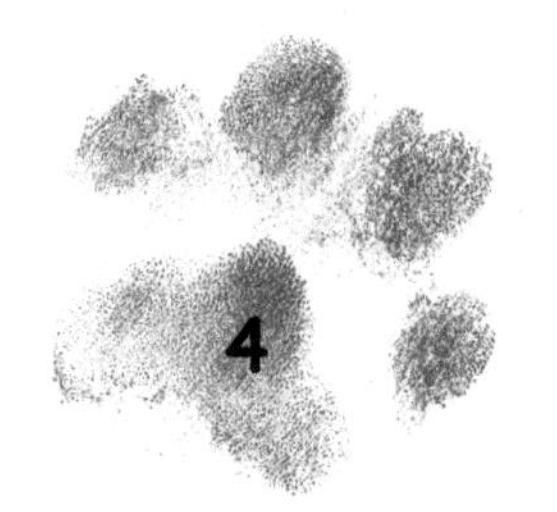

So Charlie came to live with the McDurgles. Charlie could not believe his luck! The McDurgles had a ten-acre farm with goats, chickens, seven cows, and twenty-four pigs.

But most exciting of all was that Bessie and Pete had ALOT of green grass, plenty of squirrels, and lots and lots of birds for Charlie to watch over. Charlie was so happy! Bessie and Pete instantly fell in love with him. They fed him, walked him around the farm several times a day, and let him visit with the cows, pigs, goats, and chickens.

McDur e Farm

All of this was new to Charlie, but he was SO happy to be with Bessie and Pete. Bessie would take him outside with her when she was hanging the wash. She even had a special chair where Charlie could sit and watch her pin the clothes to the line. He could see the birds fly back and forth from their nests to feed their babies.

rm

But his favorite thing to do was to sit on Pete's tractor and watch the squirrels gather acorns from the big oak in the yard. Charlie liked to bark at the squirrels. Pete kept telling Charlie to stop barking! Charlie would not listen. So Pete took Charlie and put him on the grass under the maple tree. Charlie was mad. He wanted to be with Pete on the tractor but now he would have to just sit in the grass with nothing to do.

Suddenly, Charlie heard a baby crying. He tilted his head and tried to figure out where the crying was coming from. For Charlie, there was no time to waste. He jumped up from under the maple tree and ran toward the sound of the crying baby as fast as his little legs would carry him.

Charlie spotted the crying baby, yet he thought his eyes were playing tricks on him! The baby's sobs were coming from inside a house that was on fire! Without even blinking or thinking, Charlie raced into the burning house, climbed the stairs, and found the crying baby! Charlie put the baby gently in his mouth and trotted down the stairs as carefully as he could! It was just in the nick of time. At that moment, the whole house went **WOOSH**, and the flames were everywhere!

The crying baby's mama was very upset and had no idea that Charlie had rescued her baby. When she saw Charlie come out of the house carrying her baby, she ran toward him, crying and yelling. Charlie thought he was in trouble. The mama was sobbing so hard. But she was not sad. The baby's mama was so happy to see Charlie with her baby! The mama picked up her baby and hugged her AND Charlie. Charlie did not understand. He was doing just what any, ordinary wiener dog would do.

When the mayor of the town heard what Charlie had done, he gave Charlie a special award along with a red cape. The cape had a big letter **C** (C - for Charlie) on it! They had a big parade for Charlie, and he got to sit on the back of a car that had no top to it! While Charlie was basking in all of the sunshine and dog biscuits that the townspeople were tossing to him, he heard some-one cry, "HELP!"

HELP!

Immediately, Charlie sprang from the back of the car and ran in the direction of where he had heard "help" coming from! When Charlie arrived, he saw a man who was being robbed! The robber was trying to steal the man's wallet. In an instant, Charlie jumped up and wrapped his teeth around the robber's arm!

The robber was so surprised that such a little dog had such a hard bite! Charlie would not let go. Charlie held on until a policeman arrived and took the robber away! The man being robbed was so grateful to Charlie. He gave Charlie a big hug and asked him if there was anything that he would like. Charlie thought and thought.

He asked the man if he could give him some goggles. Sometimes when Charlie would run, the wind would make his eyes water. If he had goggles, Charlie would be able to see without the wind hurting his eyes.

"Done," said the grateful man. The man gave Charlie some clear blue goggles. "Also, Charlie, I am going to put two Ws on your cape because you truly are a Wiener Wonder. Thank you for coming to my rescue!"

WW

Now Charlie had a cape with two Ws and a C on it and a pair of goggles. He was the luckiest wiener dog in the world! He couldn't wait to show Bessie and Pete his cape and goggles and tell them how he had earned them!

"Charlie! Charlie! Charlie, where are you? Your dinner is getting cold!" cried Bessie.

Charlie jumped up from the green grass under the maple tree. Was it a dream? You mean there was no burning house or robber or cape or goggles? No parade, no biscuits, or car without a top on it? But...

"Charlie," said Bessie, "where did this red cape with two **W**s and the letter **C** on it come from? And what about these goggles? How did they get here? Heavens to Betsy, Charlie. The things you come home with!"

Charlie just grinned and hungrily gobbled all of his dinner.

THE END

ABOUT THE AUTHOR

Cindy Brumbaugh is a mother of two boys, Benjamin and Bryan, and is also a retired swim coach of 23 years. Cindy currently lives in Pennsylvania and frequents Ocean City, New Jersey with her husband Howard and dog Charlie, a rescued dachshund who is 8 years of age. This is Cindy's first publication.

CPSIA information can be obtained
at www.ICGtesting.com
Printed in the USA
BVOW10s2148210316
441220BV00003B/4/P

9 781682 896150